THE GREAT RESCUE

A story about teamwork

On the busy Island of Sodor, a little boy named Josh waited at Knapford Station. When Thomas puffed in with his coaches, Annie and Clarabel, Josh looked up tearfully.

"Cinders and ashes, what's wrong?" Thomas asked.

"I've lost my kitten, Whiskers," said Josh.
"Will you help me look for him, please?"

"Of course," peeped Thomas eagerly.

Thomas, Annie, and Clarabel chuffed
around the Island. But they did not see any
sign of Whiskers.

"Where could that kitten be?" Annie asked.

Soon they came upon some stray sheep in the countryside. Thomas peeped his horn just as Farmer McColl appeared.

"Hello, Thomas," said the Farmer.

"I'm looking for a lost kitten," Thomas told him. "You haven't seen one, have you?"

"No, just my sheep and cows," said Farmer McColl. "Sorry."

Then, Thomas saw a young girl walking her dog by the windmill.

"Have you seen a little kitten?" Thomas asked.

But the girl just shook her head.

Suddenly, Thomas heard a whirring noise in the sky up above.
It was Harold the Helicopter.

"Peep, peep!" went Thomas' whistle, and Harold flew
down to say hello.

"We've been looking everywhere for a lost kitten," Thomas said. "Can you help us to look for him?"

"Of course," said Harold. "After all, I'm a member of the Search and Rescue Team!"

But even with Harold's help, the friends still couldn't find Whiskers.

"Oh dear, Thomas," Annie said. "What shall we do?"

"We have to keep searching," Thomas replied,
"even if it takes all day."

"We'll all work together," added Harold from above.

Harold flew on ahead to the Animal Park.

Looking down below, he could see all kinds of animals.

He zoomed in for a closer look.

"Wow!" Harold said. "I see lots of big cats but no sign of little Whiskers."

Suddenly, Harold spotted something white and fluffy in a leafy, green treetop. It was Whiskers!

Harold got as close to the treetop as he could. He didn't want to scare the kitten.

"Hello, Whiskers," Harold coaxed. "Jump to me."

But the kitten was too frightened to move.

"Don't worry, Whiskers!" said Harold. "I'll be right back with help!"

Harold flew off to find Thomas.

When he saw the blue tank engine, he hovered overhead. "Thomas! Thomas!" Harold cried. "I found Whiskers! He's stuck in a tree!"

Thomas knew that they'd need a ladder to get Whiskers down. Suddenly, an idea flew into his funnel.

"I think we know someone with a very tall ladder," he said.

"Yes, we'll ask Flynn to help!" agreed Harold.

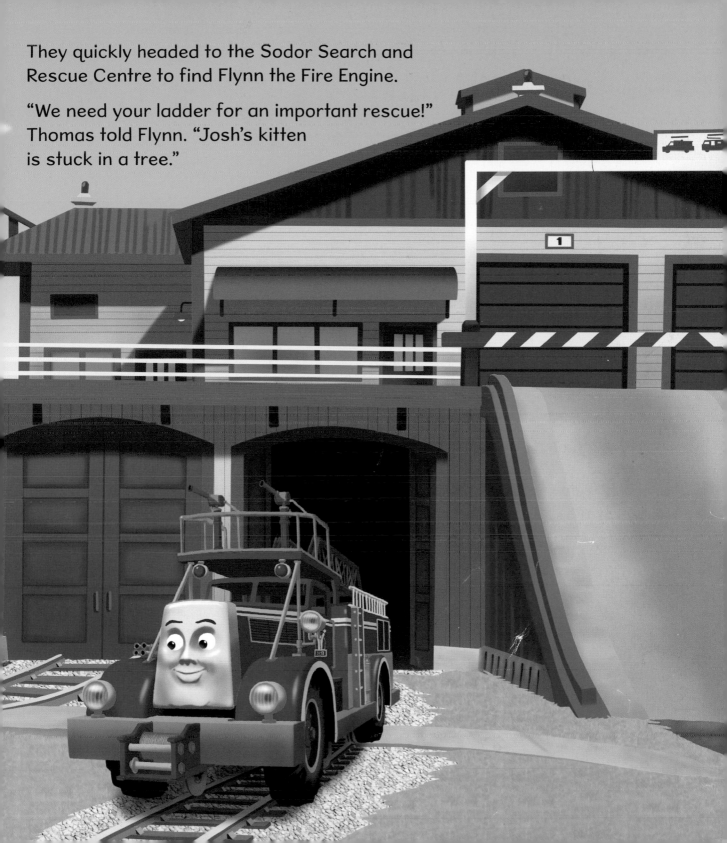

They quickly headed to the Sodor Search and Rescue Centre to find Flynn the Fire Engine.

"We need your ladder for an important rescue!" Thomas told Flynn. "Josh's kitten is stuck in a tree."

"I'm ready to rescue!" said Flynn.

Flynn, Thomas, Annie and Clarabel followed Harold back to the tree. When they got there, Flynn raised his really long ladder, and his Driver climbed up to rescue Whiskers.

"Easy does it," said Flynn.

"Well done!" cheered Thomas.

At last, Josh and Whiskers would be together again.

Annie started to sniffle. "I love happy endings!" she cried.

Just then, Bertie stopped by to see what was happening. When he heard about Whiskers, Bertie offered to drive the kitten back to Knapford Station where Josh was waiting.